LILY BOOP

LILY BOOP

by Ellen Switzer

pictures by Lillian Hoban

Crown Publishers, Inc.   New York

Published by Crown Publishers, Inc., 225 Park Avenue South, New York, New York 10003
and simultaneously in Canada by General Publishing Company Limited
CROWN is a trademark of Crown Publishers, Inc.
Manufactured in the United States of America

Library of Congress Cataloging in Publication Data
Switzer, Ellen.   Lily Boop.
Summary: A young girl describes her adventures
with her unusual friend, Lily Boop, who keeps a pet slug
and eats raw eggs for lunch.
1. Children's stories, American. [1. Friendship — Fiction] I. Title.
PZ7.S98237Li 1985 [Fic] 84-23813
ISBN 0-517-55649-9   10 9 8 7 6 5 4 3 2 1   First Edition

62946

For Jessica, Portia, Mose, Ben, and Gus

I like to sleep over at my best friend Lily Boop's house. Things are so different there. At bedtime Mrs. Boop sets the alarm clock so that it goes off every hour on the hour all night long. When the alarm wakes us up, we take turns telling our dreams. It's great fun, but in the morning I never feel as if I've had enough sleep. It doesn't bother the Boops though. Lily and her mother are always up before dawn, cutting their fingernails and toenails, which grow several inches every night. They also file their teeth to sharp points...and they don't brush them.

Lily's family moved here from the North about six months ago. Lily says they lived in underground tunnels. I asked my dad if it could be true.

"Of course not, Judy," my dad said. But after he met Lily he didn't seem so sure.

One day Lily asked me why the kids around here cut their whiskers. "We don't have whiskers," I said.

Lily laughed as if she didn't believe me. "Well, you'd all look prettier if you'd let them grow out."

Lily has a pet slug named Beth. She makes tiny paper dresses and hats for her. "Lily, do your parents let you keep a pet slug in your bedroom?" I asked.

"They gave me Beth for my birthday," she said.

"Mom," I said when I got home, "can you believe that Lily got a slug for a birthday present? I'm glad I got a radio for *my* birthday."

Mom laughed and said, "Well, at least Mrs. Boop never has to tell Lily to turn down her slug!"

When Lily first moved to our town, the other kids at school said that she looked strange. No one talked to her. I felt sorry for Lily, but I wasn't friendly to her either. I guess I was afraid that if I hung around Lily the other kids would make fun of me, too. It wasn't a nice way to feel.

For an entire week Lily had no friends. At lunchtime she sat all alone. We'd watch her eat because she had so many yucky-looking things in her lunchbox. One day she took an egg from her lunchbox. We waited for her to peel it, but she poked a hole in it with one of her sharp teeth. She poked another hole in the bottom and then sucked out the inside. "Yuck, she ate a raw egg!" we all said.

Lily ate three more eggs the same way. We couldn't believe it! She drank her carton of milk and, when she was done, she stuck the straws on her front teeth. She looked at us as if nothing unusual had happened. We all cracked up. Every kid in the lunchroom, including Lily, laughed and laughed. We couldn't stop.

"Quiet down in here!" said a teacher. "What is so terribly funny?"

We all looked at Lily and cracked up again. From then on Lily was one of us.

The first time Lily invited me to have dinner at her house I was a little nervous because I knew her family was so different. Would Mrs. Boop serve me raw eggs, onion yogurt, sugared potatoes, mushroom cookies, or some of the other crazy stuff I had seen in Lily's lunchbox? I was right. She made tuna pancakes with squash sauce for dinner. I didn't want to hurt Mrs. Boop's feelings, but I just couldn't eat tuna pancakes with squash sauce. I said, "No, thank you."

"Oh, I know something you might like better," she said. She smiled and made me a strawberry-and-olive sandwich. I knew I'd have to eat it. Actually, it wasn't bad.

I have had only one fight with Lily. We can laugh at it now but at the time it was terrible. It all started when Lily wanted to join the Prize Pets Club. Prize Pets is our club for anyone with a pet. I am the club president and my cat, Toby, is a member. We also have two hamsters, a dog, a rat, and a parakeet in the club.

Beth the slug was a problem. To tell the truth, she was sort of disgusting. But I'd never say that to Lily. Instead, I told her that slugs weren't really pets. "They're more like pests," I said. "They wreck people's gardens and leave slimy trails. Why don't you get a kitten?"

"Beth's trail of slime helps her move along," said Lily. "It also protects her from getting poked by sharp objects. Slugs are very interesting. I bet you didn't know that Beth's eyes are on the end of her feelers. And Beth is much smarter than any cat. She'll even hold still while I dress her. Toby would never do that."

"I'd like to see Beth catch a mouse," I said.

The club took a vote. No slugs.

"Well, Judy, I guess this is the end of our friendship," said Lily. "And think how Beth must feel. If she dies of a broken heart, it will be all your fault."

We didn't speak for five days.

A few days later Lily brought two lunchboxes to school. We still weren't speaking, but I was curious to see what she had in that second lunchbox. I pretended to be busy eating while I moved closer. The second lunchbox had a sign on it: SLUG CLUB. Soon Lily opened the lid and there was Beth, decorated with feathers and red stars. On her head was a tiny gold crown. I laughed.

"What's so funny?" asked Lily.

"The sight of a queen eating old leaves."

"They're fresh leaves," said Lily. "And if I told my friends in the North what you eat, they'd probably laugh themselves to death."

"It's a good thing you opened the other lunchbox first," I said, feeling mean. "Otherwise you might have taken a bite out of Beth."

"That's not funny," said Lily. Then, all of a sudden, she laughed. Then I laughed. And we both knew we were best friends again.

One day after school my mom said, "Judy, your father and I are going away for the weekend. I called Mrs. Boop and she said they would love to have you and Toby stay at their house." This was sort of a shock. Lily's house was fun, but what if I got homesick? What if I got a stomachache from avocado soup and garlic pie? I tried not to think about it.

Lily's bedroom was wonderful. Like all the other rooms in her house, a layer of dirt covered the floor and plants, and small trees were growing in it. It was like living in a jungle and the soil and plants gave off a steamy, wet-earth smell.

Instead of a bed Lily had a little nest in a corner made of soft, dried leaves. She had made one for me, too.

"I've got a great idea," said Lily. "We can make Toby some clothes tonight. He'd look great in a cowboy outfit."

"Yes, with a vest and chaps," I said, glancing at Toby, who was crouching on a branch near the ceiling. The poor guy was terrified of the Boops' house.

"Mom is out with friends tonight," said Lily. "We'll be alone. She made some tomato pudding and shrimp cupcakes for our dinner."

"Could I make myself a cheese sandwich?" I asked.

"Sure," said Lily.

After dinner we made our way through the brush in the hallway to Lily's room. Lily brought out her sewing box. I held Toby while she measured him for his cowboy suit. We were laughing, but Toby didn't enjoy it at all.

Toby looked handsome in his vest and striped pants. He also had a cowboy hat with a shiny foil star that said SHERIFF.

We made a yellow terrycloth bathrobe with a sash for Beth. I thought it looked great, but Lily said that yellow wasn't one of Beth's best colors. "Beth is a banana slug, you know," she said proudly. "She could grow to be a foot long."

I felt a little sick at the idea. "I like her the size she is," I said.

We both heard the noise at the same time: a faint claw-
ing outside the door. As we listened it grew louder.

"What's that?" I whispered.

"I don't know," said Lily. She quickly tiptoed over to the
door and locked it.

I had never liked hearing strange noises at home, but at someone else's house it was even more frightening. "Maybe your mother came home early," I said hopefully.

"She wouldn't sneak around making scratching sounds," said Lily.

The noise became louder. We could hear the cracking and snapping of wood somewhere under the floor.

"Hide!" whispered Lily. And she immediately burrowed under the dirt, creating a rounded mound as she tunneled along.

How could she have done that? I was amazed. I took a deep breath and dived into the dirt just as Lily had done. I clawed wildly with my fingers, but instead of going under, I got dirt in my eyes, up my nose, and in my mouth.

Now I heard chewing and crunching sounds under the floorboards. I jumped up into a bush, hoping the thick leaves would hide me. I sat there trembling with fear and spitting out dirt. I was terrified!

I could no longer see Lily. Even Toby had hidden, but I could hear him growling.

Suddenly there was a loud splintering crunch followed by a spray of dirt. Something appeared in Lily's bedroom! Something gross and filthy!

It saw me!

"Is this, by any chance, the Boop residence?" it inquired politely.

I tried to say "Yes," but no sound came out. Suddenly I heard Lily scream, "Aunt Thelma! Aunt Thelma, it's you!"

While Aunt Thelma was drinking a glass of chilled broccoli juice with mud dripping off her whiskers and her sharp teeth shining, I decided to introduce myself.

I climbed down from my branch. "Hello," I said nervously.

"This is my best friend, Judy," Lily said to Aunt Thelma.

"What a lovely girl . . . you are a girl, aren't you?"

I thought this was a rude question, but I smiled anyway to be polite.

"I could do with a bit of a rest," said Aunt Thelma. "What a trip! So much clay and rock. Don't set the alarm clock tonight, Lily. We'll tell all our dreams in the morning."

"I'll leave Mom a note that you'll be in the guest room," said Lily. "She'll be so happy."

As Lily and Aunt Thelma disappeared down the hall, I heard Aunt Thelma whisper, "Strange, how small their heads are...."

"Yes," I heard Lily reply, "but they all look like that. You'll get used to it after a while."

Soon after the school year ended Lily told me the terrible news. She and her mother were moving back to the North. I had never had a wonderful friend like Lily and now I was going to lose her. Lily was sad, too.

"Why are you moving?" I asked.

"So we can be with my father. He can't get work here. He maps underground tunnels, and there are lots of jobs for him in the North."

"Oh, I see," I said, but I really didn't understand at all.

"I've got a plan," said Lily. "Why don't you and Toby come live with us this summer? My friends in the North would like you. I'd tell them that you are my best friend. Then they wouldn't care that you look and act weird."

"What do you mean *I* look and act weird?"

"Well, your flat face and tiny teeth . . . the gross food you eat and things like that."

"Do your friends in the North look and act like you?"
I asked.

"Sure they do. My friend Ben can dig four and a half feet
per minute. He won first place in the National Dig-a-
Thon. And my friend Gina has a pet earwig."

"What's an earwig?"

"They're kind of like cockroaches, but even cuter. They
have hard, shiny bodies like cockroaches, but what makes
them special is a big pair of pincers on their bottoms."

"Yuck," I said.

I sure was interested, but I knew I was too scared to go to the North with Lily. I would be a stranger there. Everybody would stare at me just as we had stared at Lily. I realized that Lily was much braver than I. "Why don't you stay here and live with me?" I asked.

"I'd miss my dad too much," said Lily. "I have to go. But you and I will always be best friends. Please come visit me someday."

"Maybe someday I will," I said.

"But you'll have to let your whiskers grow out," said Lily. "All the girls in the North do."